Thescelosaurus

Oviraptorosaur

Torosaurus

Edmontonia

I'm Bad!

KATE & JIM
McMULLAN

JOANNA COTLER BOOKS

An Imprint of HarperCollinsPublishers

I'm Bad! Text copyright © 2008 by Kate McMullan Illustrations copyright
© 2008 by Jim McMullan   Manufactured in China.   All rights reserved.
No part of this book may be used or reproduced in any manner whatsoever
without written permission except in the case of brief quotations embodied in
critical articles and reviews. For information address HarperCollins Children's
Books, a division of HarperCollins Publishers, 1350 Avenue of the Americas,
New York, NY 10019. www.harpercollinschildrens.com

Library of Congress Cataloging-in-Publication Data is available.
ISBN 978-0-06-122971-8 (trade bdg.) — ISBN 978-0-06- 122972-5 (lib. bdg.)

Typography by Neil Swaab   2 3 4 5 6 7 8 9 10   ❖   First Edition

For T. McGhee Louise Steiner

Thanks to the jawsome talents at HarperCollins, Joanna Cotlerex, Karen Nagelosaurus, Alyson Dayodon, Neil Swaabatops, Jaime Morrellimus, Ruiko Tokunagastega, and Kathryn Silsandoceras, and to our kick-a-whomper Pippins, Holly McGheeotitan, Emily van Beekaraptor, Samantha Cosentinotaurus, and Cleo.

Tons of thanks to Dr. Matthew Lamanna, Assistant Curator of Vertebrate Paleontology, Carnegie Museum of Natural History, for his knowledge and his sense of humor.

I'm REALLY BIG.

6-tons-of-MUSCLE-on the-hustle BIG.
And my BIG empty belly is
growling for GRUB.

frrrRUMble

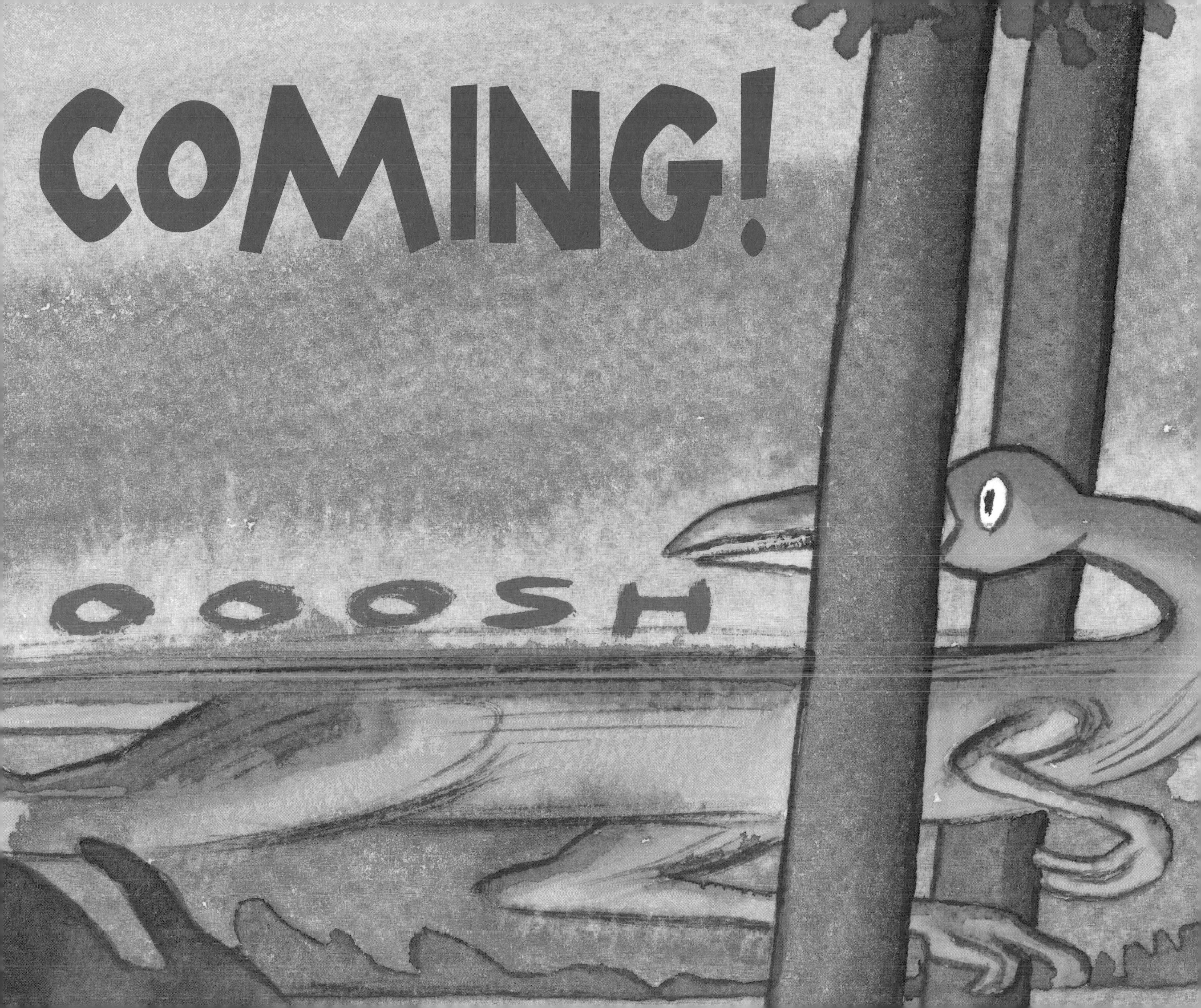
COMING!
OOOSH

I love my mom.

Triceratops

Stygimoloch

Ornithomimus

Pachycephalosaurus